Hazel, the mare, lived in the old forest stable at the base of a tall mountain. Outside the stable, a huge green meadow provided room for the other horses and forest animals to run and play and the most delicious grass to eat.

When she was younger Hazel could run like the wind, but now her legs often ached and she was content to graze in the meadow, walk along the trail and chat with her friends.

Today, Hazel was happy to see her young friend, Tippee, bouncing down the trail toward her. Tippee loved to climb onto Hazel's back and brush her mane.

As Tippee brushed Hazel, they reminisced about the wonderful adventures they had shared over the years, the butterflies they had chased and the countless games of tag with the other animals. They especially loved to remember the overnight camping trips in a special alpine meadow way up the mountain.

As they talked Hazel looked at the mountain and said, "I would love to go up the mountain again with you. I can't run like I used to but I'd like to see the colors of the meadows, smell the flowers, and feel the cool mountain air again."

Tippee started bouncing with excitement and lost her balance. Laughing as she dangled from Hazel's mane, Tippee squealed, "I would love to go. Could Spunky, the skunk, go, too? I've told him all about the meadows. Don't worry, we can climb slowly. It will be great fun."

It was late spring when Hazel, Tippee and Spunky slowly climbed the mountain. Wildflowers painted splashes of vibrant colors along the trail and the spring mountain air smelled clean and fresh.

When they reached the meadow, they quickly set up their campsite. Then all of them headed for the open field where Tippee and Spunky chased butterflies and played tag while Hazel enjoyed nibbling on the fresh clover.

That evening they sat around the campfire, happily exhausted, enjoying roasted marshmallows. When Spunky fell asleep while chewing his third marshmallow, Tippee decided it was time for them to climb into their sleeping bags. Hazel chose a spot near them and soon all three of them were sound asleep.

As they slept, the stars — bright twinkles of blue and purple — lit up the entire night sky, casting soft shadows over the mountains. Moonbeams added their special beauty to the scene.

A growing rumble woke Hazel. Looking up, she saw blue and purple horses emerging from the shadows of the mountain, racing toward her with such grace and speed it seemed like they were being carried on the wind. "The Dream Horses," Hazel whispered in awe, her eyes wide with amazement.

Hazel had heard of these magnificent horses but wasn't sure they really existed. Now, as she watched the Dream Horses run and frolic in the meadow, she whispered, "If only I could run like that just once more, it would be a dream come true." Just then a voice near her whispered, "That's why we're here—to make your dream come true. You've been such a good friend to so many, we thought we should do something nice for you. So come, play with us. While we're here you will be able to run like the wind once again."

11

It seemed too good to be true, but Hazel lost no time in joining them. For the next several hours Hazel ran and frolicked with the other horses, full of energy and free of pain.

When the first rays of sunlight announced the new day, the Dream Horses explained they had to leave. They left as quickly as they had come, fading back into the shadows of the mountain. Hazel, still amazed at all that had happened, started munching some violets that had blossomed at dawn.

Soon Tippee and Spunky woke up, not just hungry, but HUNGRY. Hazel said, "Let's walk some of the paths and find the special berries we can only get up here in the mountain. But be careful, some of the berries can give you a bad tummy ache."

As they wandered the mountain paths, Spunky ran ahead. "I found some berries," he yelled. Just as he was about to pop one in his mouth, Hazel caught up with him and said, "No, Spunky, don't eat that. It can hurt you!" Hazel pointed to a low-growing bush on the other side of the path, which was loaded with lots of purple berries. "Eat some of those berries. They are delicious and good for you," she said.

As they walked back to their campsite, Hazel stopped and said, "See that white fluffy ball? That's a cocoon. Soon a butterfly will emerge from it."

Looking at the cocoon, Tippee asked Hazel, "How do you know so much?"

"Every day of my life I have learned something, either on my own or from someone else."

"How could you learn something from me?" Spunky asked. "I'm too little."

"From you, I learned not to fall asleep eating a marshmallow," Hazel said with a wink.

When they all stopped laughing, Hazel said, "But the most important thing I have learned from both of you is how much you mean to me and how happy I am to be with you."

As the stars twinkled that night, after another day full of fun and laughter, Tippee fell asleep thinking how lucky she was to know Hazel and Spunky. And just as Spunky fell asleep he realized he had learned something really special that day. Friends come in all ages.

Dedicated to my fifth grade teacher, Judy Muehlenbeck Traub, whose kindness has been a lifeline of hope throughout the years. Thanks for teaching me lessons that make life worth living and last a lifetime.

With special thanks to:

baby, Aaron Michael Otis, whose short life reminds us of the importance of making each day precious with those we love and care about;

my friend, Jaci Hopper, who has taught me that each day is a special gift;

my friend, Nancy Madson, who reminds me to never underestimate the importance of being a special person in the life of a child;

my dentist, Dr. Richard J. Strand, whose gentleness and snappy humorous replies have taught me that many experiences can be pleasant, but a few things in life cannot be negotiated — that's just reality;

and to many close friends who remind me that life is a journey of learning and growth.